THIS CANDLEWICK BOOK BELONGS TO:

_____

_____

_____

_____

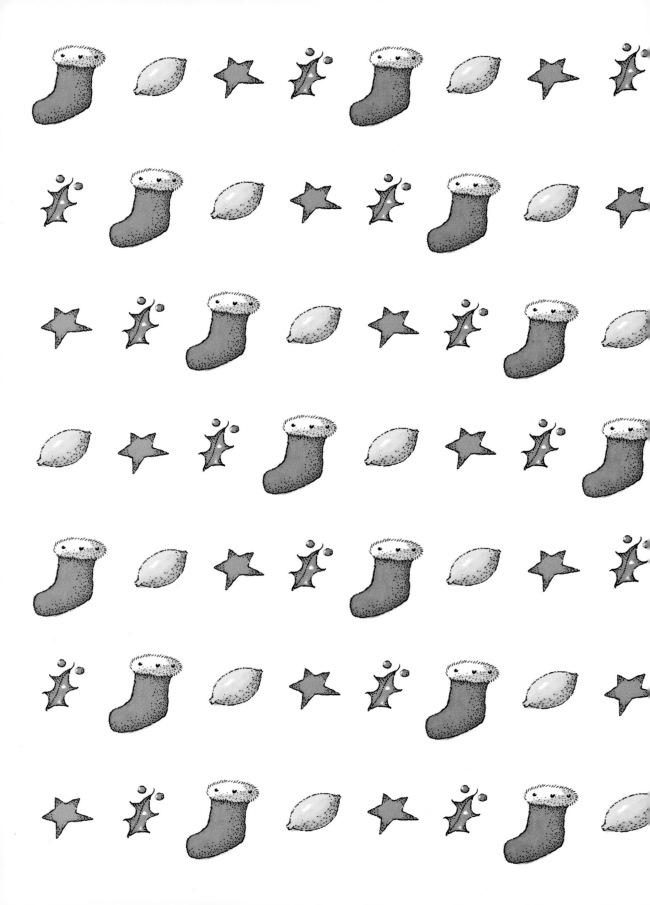

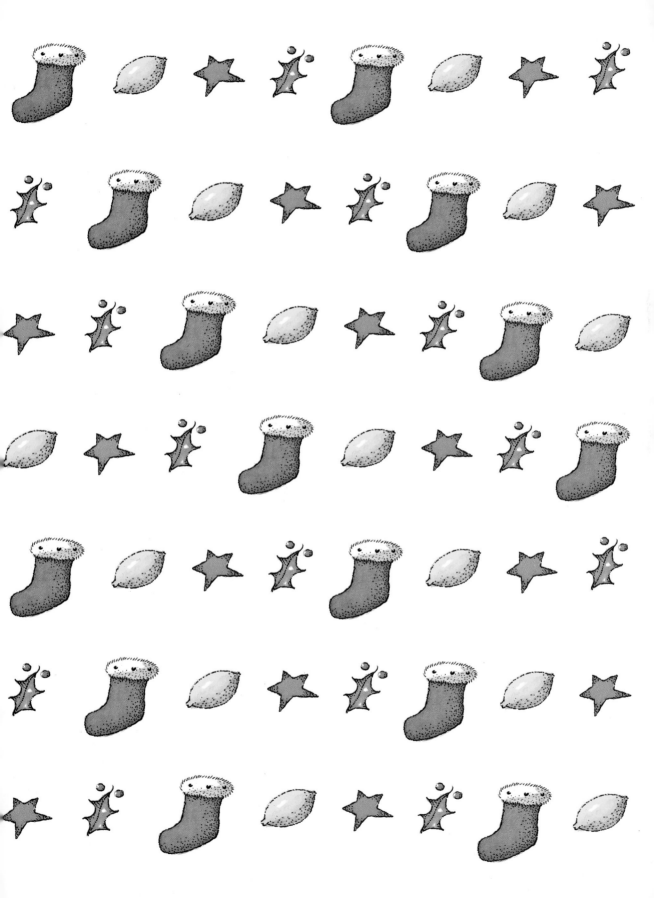

For Nancy, with lots of love
V. F.

For my mum and dad
C. F.

Text copyright © 1992 by Vivian French
Illustrations copyright © 1992 by Chris Fisher

Second U.S. paperback edition 1997

Library of Congress Catalog Card Number 95-67987

ISBN 0-7636-0349-X

2 4 6 8 10 9 7 5 3 1

Printed in Hong Kong

This book was typeset in Bookman.
The pictures were done in pen and ink and watercolor.

Candlewick Press
2067 Massachusetts Avenue
Cambridge, Massachusetts 02140

Christmas Mouse

Vivian French
illustrated by Chris Fisher

CANDLEWICK PRESS
CAMBRIDGE, MASSACHUSETTS

It was the day before Christmas.
Mother Mouse, Dora Mouse, Little Mouse, and Baby
Mouse went to visit Grandma and Grandpa Mouse.

Grandpa had a cold, but Grandma said he would be better by Christmas Day. She brought him a hot lemon and honey drink. Little Mouse loved hot lemon and honey drinks, but there weren't enough lemons for him to have one too.

Mother Mouse settled Grandpa in the comfy kitchen chair with a blanket over his knees. Little Mouse loved snuggling up on his lap under the blanket, but Mother told him to play with the baby.

Dora found some paper and made Grandpa a get-well card. Little Mouse told Dora that he loved cards, too, but she told him he'd have to wait until Christmas Day to get one.

Baby Mouse climbed onto Grandpa's lap with a book.
"I'll get a book too," said Little Mouse.
"No room," the baby said firmly.

Little Mouse went under the table to think.
He came out again and sneezed very loudly.
"ACHOO! ACHOO! ACHOO!"
"Poor Little Mouse," said Grandma.
"Do you have a cold too?"
Little Mouse nodded.
"Oh, no," said Mother.
"Achoo!" said Little Mouse.

Mother and Dora and Little Mouse and the baby said
good-bye to Grandpa and Grandma and hurried
through the rain back to their own house. There
was a letter on the doormat, and Mother opened it.
"How nice!" she said. "We've been invited next door
for dinner tonight. Even the baby can come!"
"Hooray!" said Dora and Little Mouse.

"But you can't come with a cold, Little Mouse,"
said Mother. "You'd better go right to bed."
"Oh," said Little Mouse.

Little Mouse sat up in bed,
waiting for his hot lemon
and honey drink,
but it didn't come.

He waited for someone
to come and wrap him up
in a soft, fuzzy blanket,
but no one did.

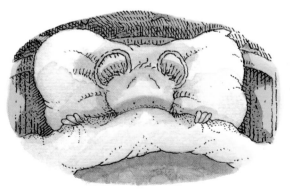

He waited for Dora
to bring him a card,
but no card came.

And he could hear the baby laughing with Mother
in the kitchen.

Little Mouse went into the kitchen.
"Hello, Little Mouse," said Mother.
"Are you feeling better?"
"Yes, and I'm hungry,"
said Little Mouse.
"Still, you'd better stay in
just for tonight," said
Mother. "You don't
want to be sick on
Christmas Day."
Little Mouse
opened his mouth to
say that he was feeling
just fine, but he
sneezed instead.

"Oh, dear," said Mother, "you
really do have a cold. You stay
here. We won't be late. Knock
on the wall if you need anything."

Mother and Dora and the baby hurried out.
Little Mouse sat at the kitchen table and felt
sad and lonely, even though the wall was so
thin that he could hear his family arriving
next door. He ate a cookie very slowly.

"ACHOOOOO!"

It was the biggest sneeze that Little Mouse had ever heard. And it was just outside the window. Little Mouse didn't know whether to hide or to go and look. "ACHOOOOO!" There it was again. Little Mouse went to the window.

"OH!" Little Mouse's eyes opened wide. Outside,
standing on Little Mouse's very own front walk,
was Santa Claus—a wet, cold-looking Santa Claus.
Little Mouse ran to the door and threw it open.
"Come right in!" he said.

Santa Claus shivered as he came into the warm, cozy
kitchen. "Brrrr!" he said. "It's awful out there!
ACHOOOOO !"
He pulled a huge white handkerchief out of his pocket
and blew his nose loudly. "I can't stop sneezing."

"Why don't you sit in the comfy chair?" said Little
   Mouse. "And if you don't mind pouring the hot water,
   I'll make you a hot lemon and honey drink."
"That sounds wonderful," said Santa Claus.
"Exactly what I need. ACHOOOOO !"

Little Mouse carefully cut
up a lemon and squeezed
it into a cup. He added
a spoonful of honey,
then turned on the
kettle. When it boiled,
Santa Claus poured the hot water into the cup
and sat back down in the chair with a sigh.

"Excellent," he said. "Thank you, Alexander."
   Little Mouse looked surprised. "Nobody ever calls me
   that," he said. "They call me Little Mouse."
"Why?" asked Santa Claus. Little Mouse rubbed his ear.
"Well . . . I suppose because Dora is the big mouse and
   Baby is the baby mouse. I'm just the little, middle mouse."

"Oh," said Santa Claus. "I see. ACHOOOOO!"
"Oh, my," said Little Mouse. "That *is* a bad cold."
He brought a blanket from his bed and spread it
over Santa Claus's knees. Santa Claus finished
his drink and sat back and closed his eyes. Little Mouse
found a piece of paper and a pencil and made a get-well
card. He put it on the table and then quietly threw the
lemon peel and seeds into the trash can.

Santa Claus was snoring—a gentle, comfortable snore. Little Mouse felt tired too and lay down on the rug in front of the fire.

His eyes slowly closed, and he began to snore too—a small, happy snore.

He was so fast asleep that he never heard Santa Claus stretch and shake himself awake. And he didn't move when Santa Claus tiptoed across the room and out the door.

Little Mouse was woken by Mother Mouse and Dora and
the baby coming home. He looked around the kitchen.
"Where's Santa Claus?" he asked.
"It's too early in the evening for Santa Claus.
 You must have been dreaming," said Mother.

Little Mouse rubbed his eyes. The card was gone from
the table—had he really been dreaming? He looked in
the trash can. The little pile of lemon peel was still there.
He smiled to himself.

"How's your cold, Little Mouse?" Mother asked
   when she kissed him good night.
"I think it's almost gone," said Little Mouse,
   snuggling down.
"Poor Little Mouse," said Mother. "I hope it's all
   gone in the morning."

Little Mouse woke up in the middle of the night.
It was very, very dark, except for one bright star
shining in the sky outside his window.
Something—or someone—flew in front
of the star and then disappeared.
Little Mouse wasn't sure, but
he thought he heard a sneeze.

Christmas Day was bright and sunny. Little Mouse's
stocking was bulging with toys and games, and he
jumped out of bed to see what Dora and the baby
had been given.

They all hurried into the kitchen to show Mother
Mouse their presents. Mother was standing at the table
looking very puzzled. Little Mouse stopped and stared.
The table was piled high with lemons. On top of the
pile was a package and a card with Little Mouse's name
on the front. He ripped open the paper and found the
softest, warmest scarf he had ever seen.

ALEXANDER

Inside the card
was a message:

With thanks to a mouse
who knows exactly how
to cure a cold. May your
whiskers always be long
and your sneezes short.
Lots of love,
SANTA CLAUS

P.S. Have a Very
Merry Christmas!

Mother Mouse looked at Little Mouse. "What on earth were you doing last night?"

Little Mouse sniffed at a lemon. "Only curing a cold."

Mother Mouse gave him a hug. "Well, a mouse who gets a special present from Santa Claus must be a special mouse, not just a little, middle mouse. I think we should call you Alexander from now on."

And Alexander put on his scarf and began his Very Merry Christmas.

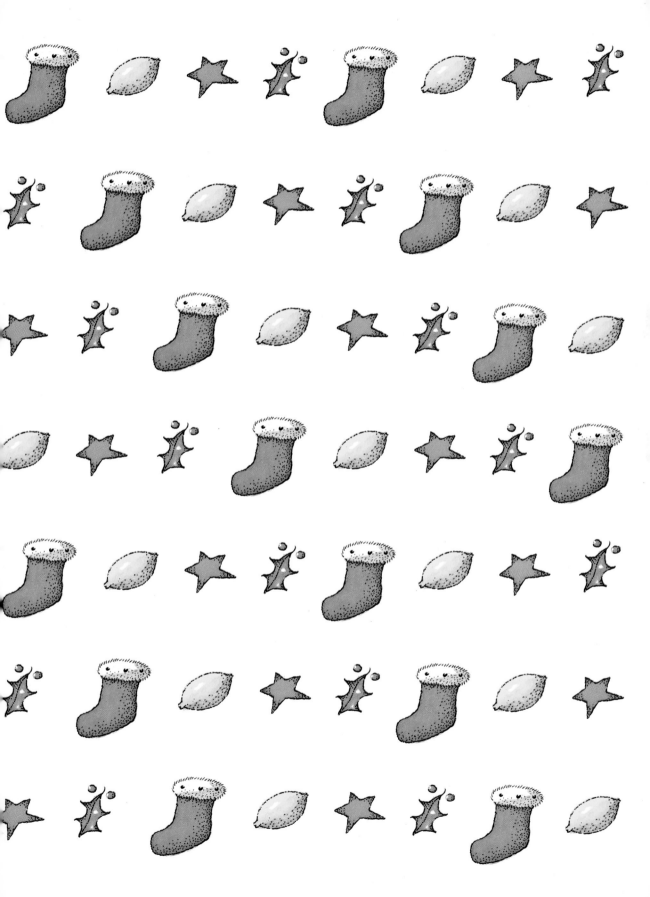

VIVIAN FRENCH has been a storyteller for more than ten years, enthralling audiences young and old with traditional and original tales. Her books include *Caterpillar Caterpillar*, illustrated by Charlotte Voake; *A Song for Little Toad*, illustrated by Barbara Firth; *Lazy Jack*, illustrated by Russell Ayto; *Once Upon a Time* and *Once Upon a Picnic*, two stories conceived and illustrated by John Prater; *Under the Moon*, illustrated by Chris Fisher; and her own abridged version of Dickens's classic tale *A Christmas Carol*.

CHRIS FISHER was born in 1958. After receiving a degree in fine arts, he launched his career as a freelance illustrator in 1987. He has since collaborated on several children's books, including *Under the Moon*, by Vivian French.